MW01168976

THE FOUNTAIN OF YOUTH

A Comedy About Three Women
and Their Quest For Beauty

By Diane Raihle

The Fountain of Youth
A Comedy About Three Women and Their Quest For Beauty
© 2022 Diane Raihle
ISBN 9798357301154

To my mom, Penny, who hopefully is watching from Heaven, who always encouraged me to pursue my writing. To all my friends who encouraged me along the way. You know who you are! To my sister Robyn and my brother-in-law Brian and Rod who kept telling me to finish it!! To my family, I did it, I really did it!!!!

The Fountain of Youth

Here is a story about three women. Most of us wouldn't really talk about this stuff. It can either make you laugh or think most of these characters need to be in jail. Not sure if we would call this a crime, so here it goes! Let's see what you think.

The year was 1979, when gas was 88 cents a gallon and Studio 54 came alive. What we all (over 60) would consider the Good Ol' Days. It was a fun time, great music and love was always in the air. We all had a great time at the discos, for sure!

Today, the early morning was crisp. The weather hadn't changed completely over to summer. It was still trying to make its mind up, hot or cold, spring or summer. The flowers hadn't wilted yet, so it was easy to say spring was still in the air.

On Long Island, down the street in a small brick home was a three-bedroom, one-bath with light blue trim around the house, where Mrs. Mary Silvasie lived.

Mary was from a Hungarian-born family in Budapest. She was the quiet type, but don't get me wrong, she could take care of herself. I heard that she once stabbed a woman with her hairpin because she was hitting on her husband. Not sure about the whole story, but I never wanted to ask.

She was around five feet four with beautiful long blackish hair with a little grey sparkling through, which was always worn in a ponytail. Never missed a Sunday at church and she loved to have her family over for dinner. She lost her husband about five years earlier to a heart attack, so she didn't really have much but her husband's Social Security, friends and family to rely on.

She was very reserved, though she'd let you know how she felt if you were not honest with her. She had two sons who lived in Manhattan, Mickey and Albert. They visited her on a weekly basis. They were good sons, in her eyes. Some may have thought otherwise. Mickey was married, with a teenage boy and one on the way, and Albert, about thirty, had never been married. We don't question that, either!

One of her best friends lived only a few blocks away. Michelle Colletti was a dark-haired Italian woman who loved to laugh and made the best spaghetti you ever tasted. Of course she did! She was very tiny, around five feet tall. Don't let her size fool you; her personality was as big as the moon!!

Mary and Michelle's family traveled to the United States around the same time from Europe to make a better life for their families.

Both families made it through the recession and they all seemed to have a happy life after that. They were both born in New York and grew up speaking Italian and English. It wasn't till later that they would meet each other.

Michelle lost her husband around the same time Mary did. It was in his sleep. We're still not sure of all the particulars; there was always a whisper among everyone about the Mafia, so of course, no one pressed the situation. Michelle didn't have any kids and lived on a check that appeared every month in her name from a bank in Italy. Again, no one questioned it, though it was just enough for her to live by. She seemed happy and content.

The third and most likely the craziest of them all was Penny. She was a New York native and was much sassier, more confrontational, but just as loyal as the two other sidekicks. They met Penny in church about twenty years ago. Their friendships had lasted through good and bad, happy and sad, sort of like the Three Musketeers, only in the 1970s, and they were all women. Penny only stood five foot two but still had a great figure for a woman her age, although she kept the Clairol box around for her strands of grey that popped up occasionally.

Penny also lost her husband a few years ago, only he was really lost. He left the house one day and never came back. Don't really wish this on anybody, it is a terrible feeling, and it took her a long time to accept his disappearance. After a few years, Penny was able to collect his pension. He was a police officer. Another one we don't talk much about. He was friends with Michelle's husband. Hmmm….

The women were now in their late fifties and still loved to enjoy life, though now the gray hair had been sneaking through and there were a few more wrinkles, and they were a bit on the saggy side, which was starting to creep in. This had them a little worried about their future and finding their lifelong soul mate. It was easy to cover the grey and work on the sag, but the wrinkles could be expensive and sometimes could make women look like mannequins. Michelle and Mary had always questioned Penny about how she still looked like she was in her forties. Penny would always reply with a laugh, "It's in my DNA!"

One night, the women were at dinner at a fancy restaurant in Manhattan, their monthly get-together. After a few drinks, Michelle and Mary began to pressure Penny again. "What the hell are you doing?" "Your skin is flawless and we want to know." Penny again answered, "It must be in my DNA," with a chuckle.

"Damn you, Penny…what the hell?"

"Okay, okay, but you're going to think I am crazy," said Penny reluctantly.

"No problem there," answered Michelle. "We already know you are!!"

"Okay, okay, okay," Penny replied. "I put other people's DNA on my face."

Michelle and Mary looked at her, like YES, she was crazy. "What the hell are you talking about?" they asked in unison.

"I…..put…..D…..N……A……on …..my…face!" Penny said slowly, as if she were talking to a two-year-old.

"What does that mean?" asked Mary, getting annoyed about it now.

"Okay, okay." Penny slowly looked around the restaurant as if she held the winning Lotto numbers and didn't want anyone to know. Then she leaned in toward Mary and Michelle and whispered, oh so very slowly, "I put DNA on my face."

By now, hearing this for the third time, both Mary and Michelle were about to punch Penny off her chair.

"Wait, wait!" yelled Penny, trying not to bring attention to the table. Again, Penny moved in closer and said, with a wink, "I put DNA on my face...." She coughed, cleared her throat...and added, "from men."

Both Mary and Michelle were wide-eyed and speechless, something very rare to see. The women weren't prudes by any means but really couldn't grasp at first what she was talking about. All three stared at each other as if they were speaking a different language with their eyes, and just like a snap of the fingers, Mary and Michelle started laughing hysterically. By now, you heard a little snickering going on around them from the patrons at the restaurant. It was an upscale Manhattan place, so you needed to keep yourself in line with the elite crowd.

Penny started to get mad and wanted them to be quiet.

"Okay! Let's talk about this later. Check, please!!"

Penny was a nurse at a sperm bank in Manhattan. An incident had occurred a few years back and she found her fountain of youth! Let's call it her "special moisturizer." She found out that she was going to be laid off and she began to panic, not because she might not be able to pay her bills, but because what was she going to do now without her *special moisturizer*?

After dinner, the women went to Penny's home to discuss in detail what Penny had been doing all these years and how Michelle and Mary could get in on the *special moisturizer*. The first question Michelle and Mary had was, "How the hell did you figure this out? How did you even think about putting this on your face?"

Penny replied, "One evening I was working by myself and stocking the shelves with vials and labeling them. I stood on a stool to put a few away in a cabinet and tripped on the step, fell to the floor and the sperm came out of the vials and fell on my face. Of course, I jumped up and was in disgust with all this film on my face. I felt the texture and it instantly felt like it was tightening my skin. After I washed it off, my skin felt very smooth, nothing like I had ever felt before. So from then on, I would steal a vial here and there to use, and I just kept doing it and really saw a difference. I couldn't stop! I'm so sorry I didn't tell you sooner. When I thought about bringing it up, I was embarrassed to say anything."

All the women agreed on how young it made Penny look. But now the question was, how were they going to collect the

"special moisturizer" without Penny
working at the clinic?

The Steal

The next morning, after a good night's sleep, the women met for coffee. Michelle thought she had an idea about how they could bottle the "special moisturizer" and start a business.

"Great idea," Penny said, "But how do you think we are going to collect what we need? Did you forget, we are not married!!"

Though the women were happy-go-lucky and fun to be around, they didn't really date. So now what…?

They spent most of the morning going back and forth with ideas. After many hours of deliberation over the weekend, it was Monday morning and Penny was ready for the first attempt to collect the "special moisturizer." The women came up with a few ideas, and this was round one.

Round one, Penny was going back to the clinic. But of course, she could not return as herself.

The type of men that would come into the clinic came from all walks of life. Most were men that didn't have jobs or were homeless in order to get a few bucks for a meal. The clinic paid a few bucks for each vial.

The women came up with the idea that Penny should go back to the facility and steal some of the vials. Since she had worked there for so many years, she knew the place inside and out.

The women thought it might be easier to dress up Penny as a homeless man so they could use the baggy clothes to hide the vials that Penny would try to steal. Yes, steal!

So the transformation began. They used Michelle's husband's clothes since he was a bit shorter than all of the other husbands. Black pants, a belt, and a flannel shirt. The coat was baggy and full of pockets. Penny's hair was long and black, so they had to be creative and put it under a hat. Since it was a little cold outside, the hat seemed appropriate. They bought a mustache and face glue and a few sideburns. After a few hours, Penny transformed into Vinny! She looked a little like Sonny Bono!

Penny decided to go on Monday morning, which she remembered was a busy day for the clinic. That way, maybe she wouldn't stand out too much.

The morning had arrived. Michelle and Mary drove Penny to the clinic and were going to wait outside in the car, sort of like a getaway car. On the way there, the women felt giddy and had a few laughs. Penny's plan was to get into the clinic, get into a room by herself, sneak out to the room where the vials were kept, and walk out. It sounded easy enough.

As they thought, the clinic was filled with all types of men. It almost seemed like they were giving something away that day. Penny walked in, trying to be nonchalant, and walked up to the counter to sign in. There stood her old boss behind the counter. Her nerves started to get the best of her. A little shaky with the pen, she signed in as Vinny Colletti, went and sat down alongside an elderly man and tried not to make eye contact with anyone.

Penny grabbed a magazine and kept her nose down and pretended to read. Peeking over the magazine like a mobster trying to case the joint to see who was where and what they were doing. Finally, after thirty minutes, Vinny's name was called. Penny sat there for a minute, forgetting to respond to that name. She jumped up and waved to the nurse; it was her, uh, him.

Just as Penny knew the drill, she was taken to a small room with a chair and a TV set with a few Playboy magazines. Once the nurse left the room, she waited just a few minutes, turned the TV on, put in a tape that began to play and nervously opened the door just a crack.

She was about four doors down from the holding room where the vials were kept. It was more like a large refrigerator with no locks on the door, and there was really no reason for it, at least until now. She knew that a few of the nurses usually took a break around 10 a.m. and went directly to their breakroom, which thankfully was in the opposite direction. The rooms were full and were typically used for thirty minutes at a time, which was one reason why the nurses took their break.

Penny slowly opened the door a bit wider, put out one foot, then the other foot, looked both ways down the hall, and off she went. When she got into the large room, the excitement of being able to get her stash was overwhelming. She was like a kid in a candy store, a bear with a honey pot and a dog with a bone...well...you get what I mean.

The vials were kept up high in a specially made cabinet. (Remember what happened before!) She jumped on the ladder and started to grab the vials, some clanging together as she stuffed her pockets. Feeling as if she had just broken into Fort Knox, she was on a high. Like a cat with catnip! Oh, sorry, had to say that!

Mary and Michelle were parked right outside, about two car lengths from the entrance, waiting patiently and seeming a bit nervous. They didn't know how long Penny was going to be, so this added a bit more to their already uncontrolled excitement. While Michelle was looking around, Mary fixed her eye on a gentleman walking down the street. He looked familiar but was too far away. As he approached, Mary frantically grabbed Michelle and squeezed her arm.

"OUCH! What the hell are you doing?" Michelle yelled.

Mary pointed at the man walking down the street. It was Mary's son Albert!

Both women scrunched down so he couldn't see them as he walked past the car. Mary at this time was freaking out! He walked into the clinic!

"What the hell is he doing in the clinic?" Mary was baffled.

By now, Penny had filled all of her pockets and looked like she had just gained forty pounds. She started slowly back to her room but decided just to walk out. As she left the registration area, she didn't realize through all the moving around that her mustache started to droop. She opened the door and right in front of her was Albert! Because of Penny being around so much while Albert was growing up, he always called her Aunt Pen. She forgot for a split second that she was in disguise and almost said hello. He gave her a quick glance with a double-take due to her sideways mustache.

Albert was a pharmacist and was dropping off a prescription for one of the nurses.

She freaked out, couldn't think, and wasn't sure how she was just going to walk out. She thought for a moment. *I can run out, but that would look like I did something wrong. Or, I can wait and try to sneak out the back door. Or I can pull the fire alarm.* Which she did!!

And, boy, was that a sight to see! Since all the rooms were filled, some of the men came running out with their pants below their knees, some in their underwear and one completely naked! Everyone ran out the front door to get away from a fake fire. Within minutes, fire engines were blaring. A crowd had gathered outside, which made it easy for Penny to slip through the people.

By the time she pushed her way through the crowd, Mary and Michelle heard the alarm. They panicked and the getaway car took off! Penny stood on the corner, looking like a bum, waving for a taxi. She opened the door of the taxi, patted her golden vials and had a smile on her face with her still-slanted mustache. Taxi drivers in New York usually see lots of crazy things, so he didn't even flinch about her looks.

Michelle and Mary went to Penny's home to wait for her to get there. The taxi pulled up and Penny paid the driver and got out. Michelle and Mary peeked through the drapes. They were excited to see Penny walking up the stairs but were also afraid to come out, not knowing how mad Penny would be. While she walked up the driveway with a big smile, the vials were clanging together, like music to her ears.

Though Penny was a bit mad that they had left her, she understood. The excitement took over and they began to count the vials. Penny gave a crash course on how to use the special moisturizer, what to mix it with and to make sure they were kept in the freezer. While they were discussing all the details, in the background, the TV was on. A loud and annoying "breaking news" announcement came on. "The sperm bank has lost hundreds of vials from a clinic in Manhattan due to a fire." All three women looked at each other and couldn't stop laughing. Penny opened a bottle of Champagne and poured the glasses. All three lifted their glasses up and toasted, "To US, to our special moisturizer!"

It's Time

Three months passed and all three women had seen a real difference in their skin. Whether they were out shopping or at church, the women would always get second looks. Their confidence was building. Penny started a new job at a small doctor's office and Michelle and Mary started to think maybe they should find a part-time job to get themselves out more in public.

Back at the same restaurant, which they hadn't been to since that day, the three women walked in together. They noticed some of the women were taking a second look at them, and most of them looked surprised. It was obvious people recognized them from their monthly dinners.

A round of drinks came and their order was taken. Penny seemed a bit nervous and jittery. Mary asked Penny, "Are you okay? You seem a bit off."

"I'm trying to think. What are we going to do? My stash is almost gone. What about yours?"

Mary and Michelle agreed. "Yes, us too. What are we going to do?"

"I can't go back to the sperm bank," Penny said. "Not after what I did."

They all agreed.

Dinner was served by their usual waiter and he too took an extra glance at the women. The women were all smiles, but now they looked a little worried and started thinking of their depleted special moisturizer.

"I guess we better start dating," said Penny.

"What? What are you saying?" Mary responded. "We haven't dated for so long! I don't even know anyone! What are we going to do?"

"I think it's time to get out of our shells," said Michelle. "What are we doing all of this for, anyway? To look good for us, or to start looking for our future?"

After a few hours of going back and forth with ideas, they decided they should venture out to one of the hot spots in Manhattan. They knew they wouldn't get into Studio 54, but there was another disco not too far away where the people who couldn't get into Studio 54 went.

Saturday night arrived and they were looking forward to a night out. It had been many years since they had a reason to get dressed up and go out on the town. With the disco scene in full force, they were excited to get out and experience the craze.

Of course, they had gone shopping for this special night. Penny wore a black jumpsuit, which looked great on her little figure. Michelle wore a blue off-the-shoulder dress with a ruffle, and Mary had the wide-leg pants, which looked like a skirt with a pretty blouse to match. They helped each other with their hair and makeup, false eyelashes, and a bit of sparkly eye shadow. They were ready! For what, they didn't know exactly, but they were excited nevertheless.

Penny didn't have a problem spending money, so she rented a limo for the night. It pulled up on time and the women rushed out and entered the beautiful black carriage. They were so excited to get the evening started that they didn't even wait for the limo driver to come open the doors for them. They all felt like Cinderella.

"Well, well, well," said Penny. "Look at us now. We all look about ten years younger."

Mary blushed a bit and Michelle agreed.

The limo driver rolled the back window down. "Where to, ladies?"

Penny replied, "Take us to a fun disco that we can get into." Back then, you had to stand in line and get picked out of the crowd by the bouncer. If you didn't have that special look, you stood there all night!

"I know the perfect place," he said. "Enjoy the bar. I'll have you there in about thirty minutes."

The bar in the limo had just about anything you could want. Penny made a Long Island Iced Tea for everyone. *Let's get this party started!*

Just about when they all finished their drinks (Long Islands are about three drinks in one), the driver said, "We're here!"

They all were feeling pretty good by this time, ready for what might be the best night of their lives.

Or would it?

They all looked out the window and saw bright lights flashing and could hear the music from outside. There was a big line at the door. They looked at each other with a worried look and asked the driver in unison, "What's going on? We won't be able to get in?"

"Don't worry, ladies. I know the owner and I called ahead. They're waiting for you. Just tell the bouncer that MB sent you."

The women were shocked and excited all at the same time.

MB stood for Michael Blake, who was actually the owner of the limo company. Someone had called in sick, so he decided to do this route. He was a very nice-looking man. Black hair, mustache, and of course, he looked very nice in his limo attire. As he opened the door for the ladies, one by one they stepped out as if they were attending a Hollywood affair. Mary first, then Michelle, followed by Penny. As Penny looked up, she locked eyes with MB and for just a moment, you could feel the spark between them. I think both were taken off-guard.

Michael quickly turned to them all and said, "I will be waiting for you here when you are ready to leave. Have a great time!"

They approached the bouncer. While everyone in line was giving them dirty looks, they said, "MB sent us," and there you had it, easy as pie! Well, pie isn't easy for me, but you get the idea. They were in!

Right about now, the Long Islands started to kick in. The women were feeling just fine. Any nerves that they had were gone. As they walked in, the song "I Will Survive" started to play. They all thought it was an omen. This was where they were supposed to be. They started to walk around a bit to find a seat, and most of them were taken. Penny saw a few spots at the bar so they quickly headed over.

What did they want to accomplish tonight? They didn't really know, but all three had in the back of their minds that special moisturizer.

As they reached the bar, they were able to find three seats together. The place was alive, with a mix of all types of people everywhere! They were only hoping they would fit in.

Penny ordered three more drinks, settled in at the bar, and started to people-watch. To their surprise, one by one, they were asked to dance. Some of the men were a bit pushy and started with a few lines to grab their attention, but other than that, they were having fun. Mary seemed to like this one guy who looked a bit younger. They had a few more drinks standing at the bar, talking and laughing.

So now, picture this, the women were drinking more than usual. Penny could hold her liquor a lot better than Michelle and Mary. At this point, Mary was flying pretty high and was having the time of her life. Her boy toy seemed to cling to her and wouldn't leave her side. They were going to take a cab back to Mary's house. I guess she was ready.

Penny kept her cool most of the night. She wanted to make sure everyone had a good time.

Michelle met an older gentleman who seemed to like her although she wasn't impressed. He started to bug her to the point that the bartender stepped in and told the guy to take a hike. Michelle was so thankful she gave him a big hug! The bartender gave her an extra squeeze. Uh-oh.

Just like that, it was almost 2 a.m. Although the bar stayed open till 4 a.m., the women couldn't last another minute. Being it was their first night out, they (well, Michelle and Penny) headed to the limo. MB saw them coming and opened the door like a butler would open a door for a queen. He asked, "Where is the third sidekick?" Penny replied, "She ran home to get her special moisturizer." Michelle couldn't stop laughing.

As the limo started down the road, little did Penny and Michelle know that Mary was in the taxi ahead of them. MB mentioned to Penny, "I think I see your friend in front of us in that cab ahead of us."

"Oh my God! Oh my God!" said Penny. "Follow them!"

Penny and Michelle jumped through the window opening from the back seat to the front seat, squeezing through and giggling all the way. They finally reached the front with MB. Penny happened to land so close to MB that she was almost sitting in his lap. Remember, the women were feeling pretty good at this time, and all the liquor had started to play a pretty big role in their speech and motor skills.

MB kept an eye on the road and the taxi in front of them. It looked like Mary's head was bobbing up and down. "Oh my God!" Penny yelled. "Look what she's doing!"

Though it did look like something out of a porn movie, little did they know that Mary was just trying not to throw up in the cab. She then stuck her head out the window and started to vomit. This was particularly bad for her because she had a partial implant for three of her front teeth. They came flying out of her mouth, as with a few other chunks of whatever…. The wind just happened to pick it up, teeth and all, and it landed on the windshield of the limo.

Well, you can imagine the laughter in the limo!

The taxi stopped and the boy toy ran out of the car as if his life depended on it. The limo pulled over and Penny jumped out like a knight in shining armor, paid the taxi cab driver, and helped Mary back into the limo.

MB drove the women to Penny's house. As he drove up, Mary started feeling sick again. They rushed her into the house as they waved back at MB. Penny blew him a kiss.

"It was quite a night!" said Penny as she walked into her bedroom, searching for some nightwear for the ladies.

Michelle took the guest room, and Mary…. Well, she ended up on the bathroom floor most of the night.

The morning came a bit too quick for the ladies. Penny was up making coffee, and one by one, they started the walk into the kitchen. Michelle shuffled across the room, grabbed a cup, sat down, and lifted the cup in the air, hoping the coffee would magically appear in her cup. Penny giggled and poured the coffee. Mary, on the other hand, came out of the bathroom with a towel on her head, still wearing the same clothes. Michelle and Penny laughed a bit, then quickly apologized.

Mary started to laugh as well. "I can't believe I was such a lightweight."

Penny and Michelle started to laugh. "Do you remember what happened last night?!!" Mary smiled (missing her two front teeth and said, "Of course!" sounding like she had a speech problem. She sat down and lifted a small plastic bag and set it on the table and said, "Would you like to share?"

OMG! Penny and Michelle laughed so hard that Michelle peed her pants! They sat around the breakfast nook and relived the crazy night.

The Party

The "special moisturizer" that Mary was able to get that night wasn't a lot. However, the mixture that Penny used, along with the "special moisturizer," was at least enough so they could stretch it out to last a month or so.

Penny started a new job at the facelift doctor. She wanted to be at the forefront of what was happening and any new procedures in the industry. No one knew about their secret "special moisturizer." The women still kept it their secret.

Michelle and Mary never worked during their marriage. So now, they thought it might be the perfect time to get out and about in the world. They started to research jobs in their area that didn't require too much experience. Michelle liked fashion so she started looking into the retail area. Mary thought perhaps a receptionist job would suit her.

Dr. Rosenberg, Penny's new boss, was a very well-known doctor, not only for his practice but for the parties that he threw. If you were invited, it was like winning the lottery. One day, Penny was sifting through her mail, and there it was:

You are invited to an end-of-summer soiree.
Martha's Vineyard, 9 p.m. until?
Saturday, August 29th

Penny was flabbergasted! She phoned Mary and Michelle to tell them all about it and they talked about how they would all be able to attend. Penny of course would bring them as her guests.

Martha's Vineyard was about a five-and-a-half-hour drive from New York, so the plan now was to drive up very early in the morning, check into their hotel, and plan for the fun evening.

***

The weekend had arrived and the women were so excited. They had planned out their wardrobe to a T. This kind of get-together was somewhat casual, but when you say "casual" to the wealthy, it's a bit different for the common folk. They all packed a few outfits so they could help each other decide what to wear.

They left around 6 a.m. to beat the traffic and to make sure they had plenty of time to catch the ferry and relax before the big night. The hotel was quaint and not too far from the house where the party was being held. However, Penny was not going to drive there. No way was she showing up in her Toyota Corolla. Luckily, the invitation had a phone number to call: MB Limo Service.

They arrived at the hotel around 1 p.m. after stopping a few times for bathroom breaks and something to eat. Due to the price of the hotel, they thought it would be better to share a room. The unpacking began and the excitement for the party was obvious. They tried to relax for the big night, and did their best to try to nap.

Penny had called the limo service for a pickup at 9:30 p.m. She didn't want to arrive too early, so she thought an entrance around 10 p.m. would be better.

After somewhat of a nap, the women started getting dressed. Penny had a few bottles of liquor from the minibar to help with her nerves. They were all feeling pretty excited. If ever there was a night to look good, this was the night.

Mary wore a multicolor wide-leg pantsuit with a plunging neck. Michelle wore a painted handkerchief dress, and Penny had an off-the-shoulder maxi dress. Perfect hair and makeup for everybody, and they were ready for the night!

It had been a few months since their last limo ride, but the excitement was all still the same. A nice young boy greeted the women and already knew where to take them. "Good evening. My name is Jeff and I am here to escort you to the doctor's end-of-summer soiree. I've heard it's always a great party! You must be special to get the invite."

The women were wide-eyed and couldn't believe what they were hearing. They filled up their drinks and all three lifted them up to say: "To US, may the night be filled with fun!"

"Oh, don't worry about that," said Jeff. "Some of the stories I've heard are pretty crazy!" The women all giggled.

If ever there was a house that looked like it should be in a magazine, this was the one. It wasn't a house…it was more like a mansion. As the limo pulled up in the circular driveway, they were fifth in line behind the other limos. The mansion looked like a castle. In the middle of the driveway was a gigantic Roman water fountain. You could also see the lights flickering from the pool that was up against the beach. There were multiple lights shining onto the mansion. You would have thought you were in Hollywood at the Oscars.

"Oh my God! Oh my God!" the women said in unison.

Their limo pulled up and a young man in a tux opened their door. "Good evening, ladies!" In awe of all their surroundings, they started walking to the front door.

You could hear music in the background. Mary said, "Listen! Is that who I think it is? OMG!"

Michelle said, "It's the Commodores!"

As they entered the front door, the room they entered looked like a disco, almost right out of Studio 54! Colored lights were flashing, but not too much that it was annoying. A few young shirtless men with very tight pants who looked like they had walked out of a muscle magazine walked up to them and handed them each a Champagne flute that looked like a mermaid. It was something they had never seen before.

"There must be over five hundred people here already," said Mary.

As they walked through the large foyer, they all sipped on their mermaids. The staff all looked like they were models from the Ford Agency. They probably were. If anyone could look like a walking mermaid, these girls did. Every single one had very long hair, blonde, black, or red hair, and all built like Marilyn Monroe.

They finally made their way outside, where the Commodores were playing on a stage lifted in the air above the pool. It was like nothing that they had ever seen before. Women dressed like mermaids were swimming in the pool. You looked a bit closer and you'd see fish swimming around with them as well. People dancing all around the pool were having a great time.

Sushi was served Nyotaimori style (the ancient Japanese art of serving sushi on naked women). Stations were set up all throughout the party. Even a few naked men were present as the hors d'oeuvres plates!

At this point, the women just wanted to keep somewhat coherent so they could check out all the excitement. Every time their mermaid glass was empty, a Chippendale would fill it up. They all started to feel a bit of the drinks starting to kick in.

So many people looked very familiar to them. No doubt they were actors, business tycoons, really the Who's Who that lived in Martha's Vineyard.

As they started to walk around, one thing they noticed was that people kept coming and going from this one area within the house. All three started to follow a few people heading in that direction. They walked down a hallway with twinkling lights on the floor to direct you to the right location. They came to this red door with a mermaid and a Chippendale standing outside. Before you entered, you were given a domino mask that covered the space around the eyes and the space between them.

After putting masks on, the women followed the flow of people heading in this one direction. Penny, Mary and Michelle were quite curious about what was happening. They came upon a group of people standing in a big circle, but because of their height (or lack thereof), they couldn't actually see what was going on. They started to push a little bit through the crowd, trying not to be too obvious about what they were trying to do.

They finally were able to get close to the action, and there was a guy in his tighty-whities kneeling on the floor and being whipped by this beautiful woman. The crowd clapped each time the woman lifted up her whip. And whammmmm, right on his butt! She was dressed in a black bustier. Some parts were see-through. She had on long black gloves along with fishnet stockings, thigh-high boots, and really long black hair that reached her butt.

All three women tried to hold back their laughter. They had never seen or heard of this before. Thank God they had their masks on, along with everyone else. It was hard to be recognized.

After a few whips, the woman asked the crowd, "Who's been naughty?" The women looked at each other, not because of the question but the sound of the voice asking. "This is a man," whispered Penny. They couldn't believe what they were seeing. He was beautiful!

They slowly scurried out of the room, trying not to be too obvious. They were amazed at how many people seemed to enjoy the show.

As they left the hallway, they found their way back to the pool area where the music was playing and people were dancing. They found a spot by the bar and they all filled up their mermaids.

As Penny started checking out the crowd, she saw someone in the distance who looked very familiar. She nudged Michelle. "Who is that over there? Does he look familiar to you?"

"Where?" asked Michelle. "The tall man in the black and white pinstripe suit, talking to, oh my God, is that Burt Reynolds?"

After calming down a bit, realizing it *was* Burt Reynolds, they checked out the tall man in the pinstripe suit.

"Do you see who it is, Penny?" asked Michelle. "It's the limo driver that took us out three months ago, Michael."

"What, wait, what?" said Penny. "It is!" She decided to walk toward Michael nonchalantly like she was looking for someone else. As she walked by him, he glanced over with a big smile, but then…he quickly remembered who she was.

As he weaved in and out of the people, he finally caught up to her.

"Hello!" he said.

Penny tried to keep her composure. "Well, hello!" she replied.

"Do you remember me?"

"Oh, yes," said Penny. "You were our limo driver a few months back." Trying

50

not to sound too rude, she then asked him, "How, ah, um, did you get invited?"

"I guess I can ask the same of you?"

"Oh, I'm sorry," said Penny. "I didn't mean anything by that. I've just never been to a party like this," she lifted her mermaid in the air, "so I'm a little nervous."

"I work for the doctor who is throwing the party," Penny continued. "He's such a great guy."

"Oh, Dr. Rosenberg," said Michael. "Yes, he is a great doctor, a very nice guy. And a great neighbor, too!" he added.

As Penny sipped on her mermaid, she almost choked on her drink at hearing the word "neighbor."

Now Penny was somewhat confused, not really understanding how a limo driver could afford a house in Martha's Vineyard, especially next door to the doctor.

She didn't want to ask, but it was killing her not to. "You must get great tips!" said Penny.

They both laughed.

Michael asked, "Did you notice the logo on the limos?" He was trying to let her know he was the owner of the limo service without sounding too arrogant. Little did she know he was also well-known in Martha's Vineyard due to being a sought-after real estate tycoon as well as the owner of the limo service. They continued some small talk and you could see the spark that had started the first time they met.

In the meantime, Mary and Michelle were sitting at the bar and enjoying the music while people-watching. And there certainly were enough people to watch!

A tall, dark-haired gentleman leaned in between them and ordered a drink. Michelle took a few second looks and couldn't quite put her finger on where she knew this man. With a questioning look on her face, she asked him, "Have we met before? I never forget a face."

He gazed at her for a moment, snapped his fingers and said, "Oh yes! I remember you! You were at my bar a few months ago and there was someone harassing you and I stepped in."

"Your bar?" she asked. She only remembered him behind the bar serving drinks.

"Yes, it's my bar. Every so often I like to work behind the bar to make sure it's running properly and my staff follows all my protocols."

"Well," said Michelle, "I never really thanked you properly for helping me with that rude guy, so thank you!"

"You're welcome, and by the way, my name is Ricky Blake. Nice to meet you. We sometimes get the wrong crowd in the bar. We just need to do a better job on our clientele."

Little did Michelle know he was Michael Blake's brother, MB, who was still having a conversation with Penny. That's how they were able to get into the bar so easily that night.

The night seemed to be perfect. Penny and Michael were enjoying each other, and Ricky and Michelle were having a conversation, but Mary, a bit restless, wandered off.

As she walked through the crowd, she bumped into a guy in a three-piece suit. He had blond hair and was very attractive.

"Oh, excuse me, so sorry," Mary said.

"That's okay," said the young man. "I'm Tim. Would you care to dance?"

After a few dances and some small conversation, Tim asked Mary if she smoked pot, and trying not to sound like a prude, she said yes. He asked her if she would like to go to his car and smoke. She was a bit hesitant but she agreed.

In the back of her mind, she was thinking: special moisturizer!

They walked out of the party and found his car not too far away, parked on the street. Obviously, he didn't take the limo here. The car looked nice from the outside (a Mustang) but once inside, it was a bit creepy-looking.

Diane Raihle

About now, Mary was a bit nervous, not sure if she had made the right decision.

Tim lit up a joint and passed it to Mary. She took a tiny hit and started to cough.

"Is this your first time?" asked Tim.

"Well, sort of," Mary replied.

As they sat in silence a bit, Tim grabbed Mary's hand and pulled it toward his pants, and pushed her hand on his already growing penis. Now she was really getting nervous and wanted to jump out of the car and run back to the party. She didn't want to give Tim the impression that she was scared. She pulled back her hand back.

Tim looked at Mary and said, "Well, if you don't, I will!" He unzipped his pants and started to masturbate.

"Let's go back to the party," Mary said, as if nothing had happened.

Tim gave her a blank look and asked her, "Can I ask you a personal question?"

"Well...huh...I guess," said Mary.

"Are you hairy?" asked Tim.

By now, Mary was really disgusted and replied, "I need to tell you that I know karate—" (she really didn't) "and if you want to continue this conversation, it will be inside at the party." Her heart was pounding and she was a bit high as well. She wanted to play it cool, so he wouldn't see how really scared she was. Her thoughts went wild. What if he was a mass murderer or put a gun to her head or a knife!

"Ahhh, you won't talk to me at the party," Tim said.

Mary opened the door very slowly and began her walk back to the party. It wasn't too far, but when she got to the front door, it seemed like everyone was staring at her. They weren't really, but her mind was playing tricks on her.

After a few minutes passed, she finally found Penny and Michael sitting at the bar. As she approached Penny, her face was white and she looked a bit scared. Penny jumped off the stool to save her from her distress.

"Oh my God, Mary, are you okay?" asked Penny.

"I'll be all right. I'll tell you later." Mary didn't want to ruin Penny's night, which was going great with Michael.

Right about now, the party seemed to be breaking up. Michael told Penny he needed to leave, the limos were starting to pull away and he needed to make sure everyone was taken care of. But before he left, he asked Penny for her phone number.

Penny, obviously without hesitation, gave Michael her phone number. He gave Penny a kiss on the cheek and walked off. "Until we meet again!" he said.

Penny was lost in her own thoughts. "When? I hope soon, tomorrow, next week, WHEN?" She gave a little wave and blew him a kiss.

About this time, they saw Ricky and Michelle walking toward them. Michelle introduced Ricky to Penny and Mary.

Neither one picked up on the fact that Ricky had the same last name as Michael. Penny was too consumed with her thoughts of Michael and their next encounter.

Ricky told Michelle it was time for him to leave so he could help his brother. He wrote down his number and handed it to Michelle. "Call me sometime! Next week!" he said as he scurried off.

Since the party looked like it was winding down, they too decided to leave. Penny and Michelle were flying high on their evening, whereas Mary, well.... Yes, she was high, but not because of a fun evening.

They walked outside and saw Jeff standing near his limo. The MB logo now stood out to Penny. It all started to make sense now. Michael was who he said he was, which reassured Penny and put a big smile on her face.

Jeff was pleasant and they made some small talk on their way back to the hotel.

Mary didn't speak much and waited to get back to the hotel to tell her story.

The women ended up talking most of the night. Penny and Michelle were excited about meeting up with Michael and Ricky. During their conversations, Michelle found out Ricky was Michael's brother. It all started to make sense now. For once, the special moisturizer wasn't on their minds. But it was on Mary's.

Back to the Work

After a day of rest, Penny was so excited to go back to work. When she arrived, the doctor left her a note. It read: *Please keep all experiences that you may have had during my party to yourself. Thank you for attending, see you next year!*

Now, that was unexpected. She wanted to tell the world how much fun she had and whom she met and whom she saw at the party. But obviously, she heeded his request, though for a full day, she felt like she wanted to burst and tell everyone about everything. She just walked around the rest of the day with a big, quirky smile on her face.

Michelle had found a job in a high-end dress shop. This was her first day job and she was looking forward to getting back into the workforce. It wasn't a high-paying job, but she was happy just getting out. Thinking about when she should call Ricky was on her mind most of the day.

Mary sat in her kitchen with a cup of coffee and was reading the want ads. She noticed this job in the classifieds: *Receptionist M-F, 9 to 3. We will train.* "Wow," she thought. She continued to read: *Sperm Bank in Manhattan.*

"Oh my God!" She started to laugh to herself. She sat for a few minutes, like she was planning an attack on something or someone. Then she picked up the phone and made the call to set up an interview. After a few questions, the woman asked, "Would you like to come in for an interview tomorrow?"

And there you have it! Mary was so excited. She didn't have the job yet, but the possibility of getting into the sperm bank…Fort Knox again…was beyond her wildest dreams. She called Michelle and Penny and left voice messages at their homes to come over after work for dinner.

She had some of her famous spaghetti sauce in the freezer, so she whipped up a quick dinner. Penny and Michelle arrived around 6:30. They sat down for dinner and began to revisit their weekend, talked about their new jobs, and then finally Mary let them in on where she was going the next day.

"I have an interview tomorrow," said Mary, with a big smile on her face.

"That's great Mary. We are excited for you!" said Penny.

"Well, guess where?" Mary asked.

"Oh, let's not play that game," said Michelle. "I'm still trying to recover from this weekend."

"Penny...you are not going to believe this!" said Mary.

"What, what for heaven's sake!" replied Penny.

"I'll be headed to where Vinny went a few months ago!" Mary giggled.

Penny and Michelle laughed and thought it was a great idea. Penny told Mary a bit about the job and how to act during the interview and gave her some pointers on what not to say. Of course, in the back of all their minds...*special moisturizer*!

The next day, Mary dressed professionally in a blue suit she had tucked away, still with the tags on. Michelle had the day off, so she was able to pick her up to drive there. It was just what they did. Always there for each other.

They arrived at the sperm bank. Mary got out of the car, turned with a smile, and waved to Michelle. "I'll be right here waiting...I promise!" shouted Michelle.

Mary walked into the sperm bank. A few men were in the lobby, not as many as when Vinny was there, but enough to make her a bit nervous. As she approached the desk, she said, "Good morning, I'm here for an interview."

The nurse behind the desk franticly said, "Thank God! We need someone like right now!"

A little taken aback, Mary held her composure. "Ah...well...I can, but I need to tell my ride." Mary ran outside, waving at Michelle. "Come back at three!" she yelled.

Michelle had the day off, so she didn't mind hanging out in the city until three.

The nurse behind the counter introduced herself. She was a pretty woman, but Mary wasn't sure about her age, fortyish maybe. In any case, she looked great.

"Hi, my name is Diane. So sorry to push this on you. It's just every time we had an interview set up, no one showed up. You are the first person to show up! We are so thankful you came."

"Wow, said Mary. "I didn't realize...."

Diane butted in. "Sit here for a second." She pointed to a folding chair in a room next to the registration desk. The phone was ringing non-stop, and the bustle of the nurses running around looked like Grand Central Station.

A bit of the nerves started to set in. "What am I doing here?" she thought. "I won't be able to...."

Right then, a very tall, handsome doctor walked in.

"Hello Mary, I'm Dr. Barone. Thank you for showing up. It's been a challenge to find someone," the doctor said.

Mary was still in shock over how fast everything was moving.

"Ah, well, you're welcome?" she replied.

He pulled up a chair beside her and asked her a few questions, then slapped both of his knees and said, "You're hired!"

Diane came in and handed her some papers to fill out. Mary quickly finished them and handed them over to Diane.

"All right," said Diane. "Let me show you the phone system. It's not too hard. You just need to know what buttons to push."

They moved over to the reception area and Diane started to show Mary the phone system. Mary took notes and it didn't seem too hard. As she was writing her notes, she heard "MOM? What are you doing here?" It was Albert.

"Ahhhh, hello!" Mary replied. "I'm working, what does it look like?"

A bit stunned, he shook his head and leaned over and whispered to her, "Mom, if you need money...."

"No, no, Al, I wanted to get out of the house and do something with my life."

"Okay, Mom, don't get upset," he replied.

Albert kissed her on the cheek and dropped off a few prescriptions. Diane ran up to the counter (she seemed to be flirting a bit) and thanked him oddly a few times.

Dr. Barone had been in the background watching Albert and Mary through their exchange. "Wow, I guess we made the right decision on hiring you. Al is a great pharmacist. We really enjoy working with him. You did good, Mary."

Mary smiled, a little embarrassed, and went back to her notes.

At almost 3 p.m., Michelle found her way back to the sperm bank and was waiting outside as promised. Mary walked out with a big smile on her face, bursting with excitement. She jumped in the car. "Well, I guess you were hired, huh?" asked Michelle.

"Oh yes!" said Mary. She began to tell her about her day and about the good-looking doctor.

All three women were now working at their new jobs and enjoying each day. Three weeks had gone by and it was time for their monthly dinner. Mary called Michelle to set up a date for the following week. They'd all been busy and hadn't stayed in touch much. Sometimes life just gets in the way.

Michelle answered the phone. "Hi Mary, oh my God, I am so glad you called."

Before Mary could even say a word, her friend said, "You are not going to believe this. Ricky called me just about an hour ago! I'm so excited, I haven't gone on a date, well, I can't even remember, it's been that long. Anyway, I don't know what to wear, I don't know where we are going, and I can't believe he called me!" she said. "He told me to call him, but he called me!'

By this time, Mary didn't want to spoil Michelle's excitement so she just listened and between Michelle's words kept saying, "That's great! I'm so happy for you!" because that's what friends do.

"Oh, I'm sorry Mary, I just keep going on and on. Are you okay? How is your job going? Are you able to sneak some of our *special moisturizer*?"

Mary laughed.

"No, Michelle, I haven't even left the dang reception desk but to go to the bathroom. Have you heard from Penny? I'm surprised she hasn't called," Mary said. "My answering machine hasn't worked for a while, so I hope I haven't missed her calls."

"We spoke a few days ago. Apparently, she has been on a few dates with Michael," Michelle replied.

"That's great! Set up a dinner so we can all catch up."

The women met at their restaurant the following week for their catch-up dinner.

Penny looked very happy, as did Michelle. They couldn't wait to tell each other what had been happening since the doctor's party.

Penny started off by asking, "How does my face look?" They all laughed, knowing exactly what she meant.

Michelle responded, "I've only been on one date, give me time!"

As dinner was served, the women reminisced on the past three months. Oh, how their lives had changed.

Someone Else

The holiday season was around the corner; all three women had been very busy. Penny was doing well at her job and continued to see MB – Michael Blake, that is! She was really getting used to the nice restaurants, the short getaways, and meeting the upscale clientele Michael worked with, partly because she was pushing the doctor that she worked with. Remember, he was a plastic surgeon!

Michelle too had been busy with her retail job. She came up with an idea to promote a fashion show, which turned out to be a big hit for the fall. Not to mention, her boss was thrilled about how well she had acclimated back into the workforce after being absent for so long.

We must not forget about Ricky. In between both of their busy schedules, they were finding time to see each other. And when I say "see each other," well, you know what I mean. No problem right now about her special moisturizer! And I am betting the same with Penny.

The phone calls still came in weekly as they checked in on each other, but they had no plans for their dinner date. They always ended with "let's check next week!"

It was Monday morning and Mary decided to go to work an hour earlier. She had some reports that the doctor needed so she wanted to get a jump on them. Since she was given a key a few days ago for the office, she now felt comfortable and more confident about her job. Dr. Barone seemed to have taken a liking to her, but Mary hadn't noticed yet.

She arrived and parked in the back parking lot as she did almost every day. A few homeless men were hanging around. She smiled and walked past. They were probably waiting for the office to open so they could deposit and get paid. As she opened the back door, the hall was dark and very quiet. She entered, closed the door behind her, and started walking down the hall. She hadn't put on the light yet. It was located up front. As she continued to the front of the office, she heard what sounded like glasses clanging together. She thought to herself, *what could that be?* She followed the sound and started to notice she was headed to the freezer, and remembered that Penny had said it was where they kept the vials. She tiptoed, step by step, and was getting closer as the clanging got louder. She reached the door, and was a bit nervous about who and what she would find. She slowly peeked around the door, and oh my God, there was Diane! She had a big duffle bag and was loading up with the vials!

Mary, not knowing what to do, turned to go back to the back door. As she turned her head, she saw the doctor opening the door.

What the hell is everyone coming in early today for? Mary thought. She stood for a second and turned into the freezer room, and Diane almost dropped her bag.

Mary said, "Quick, the doctor is coming down the hall!"

Without an explanation, literally, there was not any time, Diane put the bag in a closed cabinet in the room. They both walked out and scurried to the front office. Diane looked like she just saw a ghost and Mary, well, she was thinking...*This is why she looks so young!*

By now, all three were in the lobby. The office would be opening in about an hour. Dr. Barone was surprised to see them both in so early. Before he could ask, Diane smiled at Mary and said, "Mary and I thought it would be a nice idea to decorate for the holidays and we wanted to surprise you."

Dr. Barone replied, "Thank you, I think that's a great idea."

Wow, Mary thought. *She's good!* Diane was prepared and must have thought this out a bit, because there it was, a big box of Christmas decorations. Even though Thanksgiving hadn't arrived yet, the jump on Christmas was the plan.

The day was very busy, so any interaction with Diane was a bit difficult. With a few funny looks at each other, Mary couldn't wait until 5 p.m. She did get the report the doctor needed, which he was thrilled about.

Finally, 5 p.m. arrived, and out of the blue Diane nervously asked, "Mary, would you like to go to dinner tonight?"

Mary looked back with a questioning sort of look. "Oh sure, I'd love to." Diane then scurried back to what she was doing. "I don't have any plans, I never do!" she was talking to herself, but loud enough for the doctor to hear. He turned with a quick smile and gave a wink as he walked out the door.

Mary never questioned Dr. Barone about his family life or if he even had one. She realized now she had never seen a family picture on his desk. *Hmmmm...* For a moment, she was lost in her thoughts.

Diane came running up from the back room. "I never thought he would leave!!

He was supposed to be off today! Why he hangs around here when he doesn't have to be in is beyond me."

A few butterflies came across Mary's, well you know, not her stomach!!

Diane locked the door, turned, and leaned up against the door as if she were barricading them in. Mary watched with confusion and just waited to see what Diane was going to say. Mary was thinking, *What could she say? I wonder if she has found out our secret.*

Diane closed the blinds, turned to Mary, and said, "So let's go to dinner. We can go to Italian Cottage down the street."

Mary grabbed her purse, but now she was really confused. Why didn't Diane just talk in the office? Her mind was racing now with why this and why that. Once they were outside the building, Diane said, "I don't know if you realize, but our office has a video camera in the front lobby."

"Ah, what?" Mary replied. "Why?"

"The doctor likes to be sure we are safe and keeps tabs on the people coming and going."

Mary asked, "Is there one in the back?"

Diane knew exactly why she was asking and replied, "No, thank goodness."

A sense of relief came over Mary, remembering what Penny/Vinny had done.

They reached the restaurant, sat down, and both ordered a glass of wine. Mary was very quiet and wanted Diane to start the conversation, so she just picked up her glass of wine while Diane nervously did the same.

Out of nowhere, Diane asked Mary, "How old do you think I am?"

Mary was startled by the question. "Uh, well, uh, fortyish? Partly because I see how you get excited when my son stops in the office," Mary replied with a smile.

"Well, I am fifty-five," Diane whispered.

Mary smiled and asked Diane the same question as if they were in a duel.

Diane, a bit confused, answered, "Well I know you have a son that must be around thirty, but you don't look a day over forty-five."

Diane replied, "So I guess we better share our secrets!"

This opened the door for Diane to start her own story. "Well, remember about six months ago, we had a fire. Well, it wasn't really a fire, someone had pulled the fire alarm. It looked like a vagrant from what we saw on the video." Mary had to bite her lip and hold in the laughter as Diane continued.

"I was in the back room, in the cold room where we keep the vials, during all the commotion. People were running here and there, and someone had bumped into a cabinet and the vials were rolling everywhere! It was a gooey mess! As I was cleaning the floor on my knees, and of course, I had gloves on, I was rubbing this way and that, not really noticing the sperm was all up and down my legs. After about an hour, once all that was put away, I noticed the skin on my legs had tightened up. I tell ya, it was weird. Now don't freak out, but I thought, hmm, would this do the same on my face?"

By this time, Mary was really trying to hold back her excitement. Should she say anything about their special moisturizer stories? Mary quickly decided to wait and have a conversation with Michelle and Penny before she said anything.

By this time, the waiter was standing there ready to take their order. They both ordered and Diane continued to explain the details of how she would take a few of the vials home each day and mix them with coconut oil to use on her face. Thus the reason she looked so young.

"So, what do you think about all of this?" Diane asked. She was really trying to navigate Mary's facial expressions to figure out if Mary was going to tell the doctor.

"Oh, well, uh…it's very interesting," Mary replied. She didn't give Diane much to read in her expression.

Mary couldn't wait to tell Michelle and Penny that their special moisturizer had been unveiled! Knowing what Diane really wanted, Mary suggested that Diane should be more careful and that stealing from the doctor might not be the right plan.

"I know, I know, I feel so bad. Dr. Barone is such a great guy." Diane continued, "I feel terrible, but it's like a drug, you can't give it up! I had a burn mark on my face," she said, rubbing her left cheek, "from when I was a little girl, and this actually tightened, lightened, and made it look so much better."

"Wow, that's fantastic," replied Mary. "Well, I won't tell anyone."

Those were the words Diane was waiting for, but Mary was thinking, *Oh yes, I will, oh yes I will, I can't wait!*

Diane replied, "Thank you."

They finished their dinner with small talk and a lot of questions about Albert, which made Mary a bit uncomfortable. She wondered why Diane never offered to give her any of the vials. She certainly didn't like the idea that she didn't offer to share.

They both were pleasant to each other; however, you could tell something was amiss. They said their *good night* and *see you tomorrow*, and off they went.

Mary couldn't wait to get home to call Penny and Michelle.

Rather than tell them on the phone, Mary asked them to meet her the next night for dinner. She had something important to discuss. Hopefully they weren't too busy with their dispensers! They both agreed to meet.

They decided to meet down the street from Mary's work at a nice bar located inside the Hilton.

The next day at work, Diane muddled around the office and didn't say too much to Mary and certainly was keeping an eye on Dr. Barone, especially when he and Mary were making small talk. Mary was busy thinking about her dinner with Penny and Michelle, while Diane was a bit nervous now that the cat was out of the bag, well, the vials, that is.

The Bailout

Finally, the day came to an end. Mary arrived at the bar before Michelle and Penny, got a small, round table and sat waiting patiently. The hotel was very busy. It looked like a convention was going on.

They both arrived, wondering why Mary needed to meet so desperately.

Mary waved at them as they walked in.

"I thought you would never get here!" said Mary.

Michelle sat on one side and Penny on the other.

"You're not going to believe this!" Mary proceeded to tell them about what had happened, how Diane had found their special moisturizer and was stealing for a few months, and about the vagrant that was caught on camera. A few giggles followed, but now there was concern and a bit of jealousy that someone else had found out their secret.

"I realize that you are not that concerned because you both have someone to fill your needs right now. However, we need to do something!" Mary said. "What should I do?"

Penny suggested telling Dr. Barone so Diane would get fired. But Mary was not that type of person. "Perhaps you can be discreet and tell him that you think you need a video camera in the hall. That way, he will be able to see for himself. But be sure to tell him, not the staff."

"We need a plan!" said Penny. "I think we need to start thinking about bottling this and somehow selling it before someone else does! You know, I work with Dr. Rustenburg. Maybe he could help us."

Before Penny could finish, the waiter asked for their order. She waved him away.

"So how the heck do you start up a conversation?" Mary asked. "'Oh, Doctor, we found something that helps tighten skin and helps reduce wrinkles. Better than anything that is on the market.' 'Oh, and what would that be?'" she said, mocking how the doctor would reply.

"This is so frustrating. We need to figure this out," said Penny.

They were so busy engulfed in their own conversation that they didn't realize how the bar had filled up with men. The waiter came over and asked if they wanted something to drink, and mentioned that the men *over there* (pointing to a table of four men sitting together, all of whom looked like used car salesmen) wanted to buy them a drink. Surprised and somewhat confused, they all said *thank you* and proceeded with their orders, not really wanting to be interrupted but staying gracious nevertheless.

The women were in deep conversation when the men decided to come over and introduce themselves. Not really wanting to be bothered, they all were cordial. The women didn't realize the men were trying really hard to get them to pay attention to them. For whatever reason, because they were from out of town and pretty naive and they were the only women in the bar, the men thought they were hookers. As the men leaned over their table, they told them they were from out of town and would like some company to show them the town. Penny, at this point, was getting annoyed.

"Excuse me, but we're not interested. You couldn't afford us!" Penny said jokingly.

Jumping in on the joke, Michelle started to pipe in about how much they would cost. The men looked excited like they were going to have a great few hours ahead of them. After a few minutes of banter, all of a sudden, the man sitting behind their table stood up and said, "Excuse me ladies, you will have to come with me downtown." As soon as the men heard that, they hurried out the back of the bar.

Little did they know that this particular bar was known for where the women of the night would hang out. Especially when there was a convention in town.

"Downtown?" they all asked. "What for?" Penny questioned the man. "Who are you, anyway?"

At this point, he flipped his badge at them and said, "Please step outside."

Mary said, "Is this a joke?"

"No, ma'am," said the plainclothes officer.

All three were escorted outside and put in the back of a police car. And of course, all of them were visibly upset. Penny kept telling the officer, "This is a mistake. We were joking!"

The officer didn't pay too much attention to them and continued to drive. Once they reached the precinct, the women were escorted into a room. All were given the opportunity to call someone. It was only 7 p.m., so no matter who they called, at least it wasn't in the middle of the night!

As they sat there trying to figure out whom to call, Mary said, "I can't call Albert, I don't want him to know anything."

Michelle piped in, "I don't know anyone except my boss, and I don't want to try and explain this!"

While the women were complaining, Mary had been stumbling through her purse and Dr. Barone's business card fell out. On the back, it had a number with the words "Call in case of an emergency."

"I guess I can call Dr. Barone? I'm sure he will be able to help us."

A police officer stepped in and asked who was going to be the first to make their call. Mary stood up.

The call was made, and Dr. Barone came to the rescue. Little did Mary know that Dr. Barone was well-known at this precinct, mainly due to the fact that the clinic wasn't too far and he was friends with a few of the police officers. So the women really lucked out. They didn't have to call a lawyer; Dr. Barone explained the mishap and the women were let go.

As they all grabbed their belongings, Dr. Barone invited them to dinner, which sounded great, since they didn't get to eat.

During dinner, everyone was a bit more relaxed. They enjoyed the small talk and a lot of giggles. Dr. Barone was fairly new at the clinic, so he didn't know that Penny used to work there. It was probably for the best so no one was recognized, especially if they were to check the video.

Michelle and Penny kept an eye on Dr. Barone and checked out how he paid special attention to Mary. Michelle eyed Penny and looked at the front door as she summoned her outside. Penny knew what Michelle was trying to say.

As soon as the check came, Dr. Barone grabbed it and said, "Dinner is on me."

Both Penny and Michelle stood up and said, "Thank you so much, and thank you for bailing us out! We both have to get up early for work, so if you don't mind, we will bow out."

Penny continued, "Mary, you okay getting home?" Penny's plan was to see if the doctor would step in, and of course he did!

Mary gave a *thank you* smile to Penny as she watched the women walk out of the restaurant. Penny looked back and gave a little wave as if to say good luck.

"Dr. Barone, I don't know how to repay you!" said Mary. "First off, my name is Paul, and it really wasn't a big deal. Actually, it really made my night. Penny and Michelle are lovely people and I can see why you stayed friends this long."

Dessert came and for now the conversation was light and cheery. Mary went into more detail about her relationship with the women and her past life with her husband, her kids and their families. This was Mary's perfect chance to find out a bit more about the doctor.

"So enough about me," she said. She was feeling a bit shy, but she wanted to know more about him, so she asked, "Do you have a family?"

"I have a daughter," he replied.

Mary's heart dropped. *NOOOOOOO!*

"She lives in California with her mother," he added.

Oh crap!! He's married.

"We don't see much of each other since the divorce," he continued.

Oh yeah, oh yeah! Mary was now pretty, pretty happy.

"I'm sorry to hear that," she said (although she was not really). Now the conversation was more about the doctor's past and how he was hired to run the sperm bank.

You could tell the sparks were flying that evening and both of them kept it under wraps, just giving each other a little bit here and there about the possibility of seeing each other again. They didn't realize how much time had flown by. Then Dr. Barone looked at his watch.

"Well, we better call it a night," said Dr. Barone.

Did you just say let's spend the night!?

"You have a mean boss; you better not be late tomorrow!!" he continued. They both laughed.

"I really appreciate you coming to our rescue, I can't thank you enough," said Mary. She stood up and gave the doctor a hug.

OH MY, this feels good. Her head was about to explode!

"Did you drive in today?" asked Dr. Barone. Sometimes, Mary would take the train in a few days a week to work and drive her car the remaining days. This particular day she happened to drive in.

"Oh, thank you, I have my car in the parking garage."

"Mary, I will walk you to your car. It's after 11 p.m. and I don't want you to

run into any night creatures." The doc
smiled.

Long Weekend

The next day, everyone went to work as if nothing had happened. Penny was bright and cheery and Michelle was getting ready for her fashion show coming up in a few months.

The sperm bank happened to be very busy, but Mary and the doctor were still able to exchange smiles throughout the day. Diane was running around like always and found a moment to whisper to Mary.

"Have you seen my duffle bag?"

Mary, with a puzzled look, replied, "No. I don't know where it is."

"I wonder if the cleaning people saw it and threw it out….I'm so upset!" Diane said as she scurried away.

Now Mary was wondering herself. *Where could it have gone? Maybe the doctor does have a camera back there that we don't know of. Maybe he saw Diane all this time!*

Right about then, after she thought about all this, she heard Diane and the doctor having a heated conversation. "Why me?" she heard Diane say. Mary couldn't quite make out what the doctor was saying, but she heard Diane getting upset. She packed up her things and the doctor escorted her out the front door.

Mary was trying not to pay too much attention but she heard a phone call being made to HR about hiring a new nurse. Mary was trying to stay out of what was going on and not bring attention to herself.

Dr. Barone walked up to the counter and said, "We will be getting a new nurse this afternoon."

Mary didn't ask any questions, however, she was relieved that Diane was gone. Especially when she didn't offer to share her vials!

The day was like any other day, busy until 5 p.m. The new nurse arrived around 2 p.m. and was very nice and thankful for the hire. Her name was Paula and she was around fifty years old but happened to look sixty! No special moisturizer for her!

Mary found a handwritten note on her desk: "Would you like to go to dinner Friday? I will pick you up after work." It was signed "Paul." As she was reading the note, the doctor just happened to walk by... Mary smiled and shook her head YES!! *Hell Yes! Her head exploded!!*

It was Wednesday, so it wasn't too long to wait for her evening with the doctor. The first thing when Mary got home, she called Michelle and Penny to tell them about what happened: Diane getting fired and her date coming up. Thank goodness both of them happened to be home, which was unusual, and both were happy for her as they all joked about their special moisturizers coming easy these days.

It was Friday morning and Mary decided to take the train to work so she didn't have to bother with traffic going home. Since the doctor was going to pick her up after work, she thought it would be quicker to go home to get ready.

I wonder where we're going? Am I going to have sex? What should I do? All these crazy but fun thoughts were going through her head during the ride in to work.

It was a normal day, busy as always, and Paula seemed to fit right in with the other staff. No one had paid any attention to what was going on between the doctor and Mary. It was probably better that way for now.

As Mary headed for the door to catch her train, the doctor scurried over and opened the door for her and whispered, "Pack for a fun weekend, if that's okay with you?"

What, wait, what? She was taken a bit off-guard but still answered YES!! *Holy crap, yes!*

When she arrived home, there was not too much time to get a small bag and pack a few things. She called Michelle and Penny to let them know, but she wasn't sure what clothes to bring. After a few suggestions from them both, she finished packing and the doctor called to let her know he would be there in about thirty minutes. Excited but a bit scared, Mary sat on her sofa and waited for the doorbell to ring.

Mary heard a car pull up and peeked out her drapes to see the doctor in a new Porsche. Her heart was pounding, but nevertheless she tried to keep her composure. The doorbell rang and the prince was standing at the door! Maybe not on a white horse, but a black Porsche will do!

He grabbed her suitcase and as they walked to the car, the doctor said, "I'm hoping you weren't thinking I was a bit pushy about the weekend, but I had this weekend planned to go to Martha's Vineyard and I thought it would be nice to have company."

"To be honest, I was a bit caught off-guard, but I am excited to be here, well…. Uh… happy to be here!" she replied, not wanting to sound too excited, but her heart was beating double-time.

The car's interior was beautiful, all white leather and all the bells and whistles for an upscale car. It was a very nice day so he lowered the roof. Mary had her hair in a ponytail, so no problem there with her hair blowing around.

After the ferry ride, it was an hour or so when they were getting closer to their destination. What was weird was that it sure looked familiar. As Mary was looking around from house to house, suddenly the big house that the women attended the party at, Dr. Rosenthal's place, was right there! As they passed the house, she didn't say anything and kept that night to herself. At least for now.

As they drove down this long street, they pulled up to this beautiful house, quietly tucked away at the end of a private road. "Welcome to my home away from home, Mary," said the doctor.

As Mary looked around, she saw a beautiful house that was connected to a large deck. Off to the right of the home was another home. It looked like what they would call a guesthouse connected to a two-car garage.

The doctor finally came to a stop, and he asked Mary if she would like to take a quick walk around the property. He seemed proud to show off the walkway to the water and all the greenery surrounding the property. It was picturesque.

After a few stories from the doctor on the history of the property, they entered the home. She thought the outside was nice, though once she walked into the home, the décor was over the top. It made you feel comfortable like you were at home. The house wasn't as large as most of them that she saw on the drive up there; however, it did have four bedrooms, a living room, a dining room, a sunroom, inside/outside pools, a big kitchen, and a few bathrooms here and there. It sat on around five acres.

I wonder how he is able to afford all this.

As the doctor showed Mary the tour of the house, there was a knock at the door. It was surprising to Mary that someone was there. She did remember seeing the house off to the right; maybe someone lived there. The doctor opened the door and there stood a young man somewhat familiar-looking, but she couldn't place his face right away.

"Hi, Doc," said the young man. "I noticed you pulled in a while ago. Will you need my services this evening?"

"Thank you, Jeff, we are good for tonight. But come pick us up tomorrow for the party around 7 p.m."

Party? Jeff? Oh my God, it's the guy who drove us to Dr. Rosenthal's party? What...how does he know him? Mary's head was exploding with questions.

"Jeff, this is Mary, my guest for the weekend." The doctor waved Mary over.

"Hello!" said Mary. She didn't want Jeff to recognize her, but it was no problem, he didn't.

"Glad to meet you, Mary." He reached out to shake her hand. "I will see you later, Doc!" Jeff said on his way out the door.

As the doctor shut the door, he told Mary that Jeff was the son of one of his closest friends who lost his life in Vietnam. "I wasn't ever in the military; however, a few of my friends were, and most of them lost their lives. I just wanted to help in some way. Growing up without a dad is painful. He's been working for me. He lives in the guesthouse and takes care of my property while I'm gone, and he also works part-time for another friend of mine. He's a good kid."

"Wow," Mary replied. "Such a nice person that you are to be able to give so much."

As if he was reading her mind, Paul mentioned, "Why don't you go upstairs and pick a room you would like to stay in? Freshen up? Not that you need to, but we are going to dinner in about an hour, if that's okay?"

"Oh, sure," Mary replied. "Great idea!"

She walked up the spiral staircase and saw a room that had windows around the whole room. It had a beautiful view of the ocean. All she could think of was *I'm in heaven!*

Paul was a gentleman and didn't want Mary to feel threatened in any way this weekend. He took the room down the hall and both of them unpacked and got ready for the evening.

After a quick shower, Mary picked a white pantsuit, her hair still in a ponytail. She was ready to go.

They met downstairs and off to dinner they went. They jumped into the Porsche and zoomed away.

He drove around, showing her some of the fancy houses and who lived where, dropping some big names, some of which Mary heard of and some she didn't. They pulled up to this quaint restaurant.

Since it was early December, the restaurant was decorated for Christmas.

When they walked in, everyone was fawning over the doctor.

He must tip well!

They sat in the corner with a great view of the ocean, and Dom Perignon was already on the table. The doctor ordered for them, a three-course meal, and Mary felt like a princess.

The conversation all night was mostly about their past. The doctor learned about Mary's husband and Mary found out about his divorce. It sounded like his ex-wife was more of a gold digger and found someone who had more of the dig!

For the first time in a long time, Mary felt like a schoolgirl on her first date. The bottle of Dom was way too good. Mary was now more comfortable than she had been in a long time.

The check never came, which Mary thought was unusual, but she didn't question it. As they walked out of the restaurant, there was a picture on the wall with the doctor, Frank Sinatra and Dr. Rosenthal. Mary glanced at it, but didn't realize who was who. The Dom started to kick in.

As they drove back to the house, the night was crisp and the stars were out. It couldn't have been more perfect.

The doctor opened the car door and as they walked to the front door, the doctor said, "Mary, I really enjoyed tonight. You're a beautiful woman and I'm hoping we can continue to see each other!"

I'm here, I'm here, of course yes! Mary's head took over.

They stopped at the front door and the doctor leaned in to give her a kiss as if he was saying goodbye and leaving. Mary couldn't wait and took the offered kiss. The little kiss started to spark the fire! Neither one could stop their feelings. He lifted her up to carry her over the threshold while still kissing her, walking up the spiral staircase.

He carried her to his room, which was the largest bedroom in the house. It was decorated to be very masculine; the wood was mahogany throughout the room, but with a touch of the home feeling like he had throughout the house.

They dropped onto the bed still locking lips, but now, started to help each other with their zippers. The doctor took a small break from a kiss and asked Mary if it was okay that they continue. Mary spoke into the doctor's mouth, "Yes, yes, but it's been a long time for me!"

The doctor replied, "Me too."

As they began, the lights dimmed automatically and music began to play. What was ironic was that *Please Let Me Show You* by Gloria Gaynor was playing. I guess Gloria Gaynor was watching out for her!!

Now they were both in a heated state, one trying to please the other, the doctor kissing Mary's stomach and traveling downward. It didn't take long for Mary to reach the heavens! Feeling bad it was so quick for her, she turned over and started kissing the doctor's stomach and started traveling downward. As expected, the doctor was ready, hard and willing!

Though it had been a long time for Mary, she didn't forget. She began to softly kiss around and around his penis, licking from side to side and up and down. The doctor couldn't hold on any longer and she helped him along the way to the big release. His big volcano had erupted! Mary couldn't believe how much; she began to wipe his penis on her face to get some of the drippings. She hadn't had her special moisturizer for some time now. The doctor looked a little puzzled but was too far gone with his orgasm.

The Big Reveal

Mary slowly opened her eyes and noticed the doctor was gone. She was a little nervous until she smelled the coffee and the bacon. She quickly ran back to her room and put on jeans and a nice shirt, a little makeup and her hair back into a ponytail.

As she walked down the staircase, she heard soft music and the doctor singing along to Marvin Gaye. She sat on the end of the stairs for a moment, without him knowing, just to listen for a moment. Almost in tears, she was feeling thankful at this moment.

Breakfast and conversation were wonderful. She heard more details about the doctor's life, which she found very interesting. But still she couldn't figure out how he could be affording all this. It wasn't her place to ask.

The doctor told her they would be going to dinner tonight at his partner's house around 6 p.m. He was having a private dinner party. Thank goodness she brought her off-the-shoulder dress that would be perfect.

The day was filled with fun, riding bikes around his property and ending in the heated pool for a quick swim before they got ready for another exciting evening.

They both were dressed almost at the same time and met each other at the top of the stairs. Mary was in her off-the-shoulder dress and the doctor was in a white pullover with black pants. Both of them were extremely attractive to each other. The doc grabbed her hand and they walked down the stairs together. Right before they reached the last step, Jeff opened the door. "Hey Doc, I'm here!"

As they approached the limousine, Mary noticed the logo MB. The drive wasn't too far, and there again was the house that looked like a castle. She didn't want to tell the doctor that she had been there before. She wanted to keep all the things about that night to herself.

It wasn't as busy as that night since it was a dinner with what she thought were close friends. The house was decorated in Christmas décor and again, it was like it a magazine. Jeff opened the door and said, "I'll be here if you need me." They thanked Jeff and proceeded to the front door. It was much more businesslike this time. Hors d'oeuvres and cocktails were passed around from waiters and waitresses dressed in black and white, the normal garb. Music was playing throughout the house through the surround sound.

The doctor wanted to give her a tour, and she didn't have the heart to tell him she had been there before.

Because of the tour, Mary didn't notice the people coming in. An announcement was made that dinner was ready. They started to walk back and find a seat.

The table was set exquisitely. Again, like out of a magazine. All the right things to have were on that table. As they sat down, Mary started to look around at who was there. Thirty people on each side of the table was something to see. Down at the end, she thought, *What???? Wait???? Oh my God!!*

Penny was there with Michael. She started to wave, trying not to be noticed. Penny looked up and saw Mary. She looked at her with such surprise. They stayed put, though, not to cause a distraction. Looking around, on the other side, she quickly noticed Ricky Blake and right beside him was Michelle.

What the hell?

She tried to get Michelle's attention, but Michelle was in a deep conversation with the person sitting next to her.

Dinner was served and light conversation was had among the guests. Finally, Penny, Michelle and Mary found a moment to lock eyes together, all while keeping their cool.

As the dinner came to an end and the plates were removed, everyone was given a small package wrapped in money. Now, this was something to see.

Dr. Rosenthal clicked his glass to make his announcement. "This gift is for you. Let me know how you like it."

Everyone started to open the package at the same time and there in the small box lay a small glass that looked like a fountain. How they made it was out of the ordinary. Penny, Mary and Michelle looked back and forth at each other and picked up the bottle that said *The Fountain of Youth*!

"I would like each and every one of you to try our new product line. It will be launched in January. You are the first to receive it before it hits the stores. Dr. Barone and I…"

What? Wait! thought Mary, Penny and Michelle at the same time.

"Welcome you to our product release party. I hope that you will enjoy it, and if you are interested in investing, let us know. We think this will take the market by storm. Per our trials, it is simply amazing!"

As Dr. Rosenthal ended his statement, Penny pulled out the bottle, turned it over, and in small lettering, it said: *Ingredients: Water, coconut oil and natural DNA.*

Diane Raihle

About the Author

Diane Raihle was born in New York raised in California and found her way back to the East Coast, living in Virginia Beach. Being a daughter, sister, wife, and mother keeps her busy. From being a DJ during the disco era and being in community theater, along with her acting career, she's had a very creative way of expressing herself. Her life has been filled with fun and laughter, one reason she has created *The Fountain of Youth*. Some parts of the story did actually happen!

Made in the USA
Las Vegas, NV
21 December 2024

15116154R00066